Stealaway

Stealaway

K. M. Peyton

Illustrated by David Wyatt

Cricket Books
Chicago

For Hal and Elizabeth

First published in the U.K., 2001 by Macmillan Children's Books, London

Text copyright © 2001 by K. M. Peyton
Illustrations © 2001 by David Wyatt
All rights reserved.
Printed in the United States of America
Designed by David Msseemmaa and Ron McCutchan
First American edition, 2004

Library of Congress Cataloging-in-Publication Data

Peyton, K. M.
    Stealaway / K. M. Peyton ; illustrated by David Wyatt.— 1st American ed.
        p. cm.
    Summary: Nicky moves to an old castle in Scotland with her mother, a horse trainer, and becomes involved with ghosts from some five hundred years in the past.
    ISBN 0-8126-2722-9
    [1. Horses—Fiction. 2. Ghosts—Fiction. 3. Scotland—Fiction.] I. Wyatt, David, ill.
II. Title.
    PZ7.P4483St 2004
    [Fic]—dc22

                    2004006176

Stealaway

Chapter 1

IT WAS A long journey. I was asleep when my mother said, "It's not far now. Take an interest, Nicky—our new home."

Out of the car window I saw thick, forbidding forest with crags rearing above, and a stream rushing through a gorge below.

"Ugh!"

I shivered.

It was a far cry from Croydon, our last place.

My mother is a tough lady called Pearl. She takes jobs with horses, quite quickly gets tired of them, and moves to another. I follow, of course. In ten years I have lived in an amazing number of homes.

"But Scotland, eh? We've never tried Scotland before, have we?"

I hate new starts. A new school. New friends. Just when I get used to it and start making a few friends, she ups sticks again.

"A castle, this time. Mr. Robson, an American owner, a multimillionaire! And a son your age. Brilliant, eh?"

She had applied for the job by telephone and been given it without an interview. Watching the landscape, I thought that probably no one else had been stupid enough to want it. Living here!

The American had sent photos. He was tall and handsome in a weary-looking way, wearing a cowboy hat and checked shirt and jeans. He said he wouldn't be there all the time, but he had two valuable mares and was going to buy a stallion. Only three animals to look after.

"A doddle," Ma said.

The last time she had had six horses, all on her own, and we had lived in a caravan. It was awful. The caravan was freezing and the yard all mud. For once, I was glad to hear we were moving on. But this place—Scotland . . . in the dusk it didn't look very friendly, to say the least. Not a light to be seen anywhere, nor a soul on the road.

The road, rough and narrow, wound uphill, closed in by forest. The sky was gray, and a few flakes of snow bobbed across the windscreen. Yet it was April, almost spring.

"The sea is just a couple of miles away," Mr. Robson said. "Great cliffs, all turf, wonderful riding."

O.K., but not *friendly*, I thought. Frightening, more. You could get lost in forest like that, so dark and thick and high. The cliffs might be a bit better. In the headlights a signpost pointed: *Hanging Law*.

"We're on the right road," Pearl said. "He said two miles beyond the Hanging Law sign."

It was called Bloodybow Castle. Rather rude. I hadn't got used to saying it yet. So far no one had asked me where I lived, but they probably would soon. Hanging Law and Bloodybow . . . not very homely. A bit different from 6 Laburnum Road. What on earth is a place called Bloodybow Castle going to look like?

It was at the end of the road, standing athwart, demanding the visitor to stop. It was massive, with high stone walls and towers, and chimneys in tangled shapes against the

lowering sky. Crags rose up steeply behind, and trees encroached from the lower hill-side. There was not a light to be seen, nor anybody to welcome us.

"H'm," said Pearl.

When she stopped the engine, the silence was profound.

"It's horrid," I said. I shrank down in my seat.

"Wait here. I'll go and see."

Pearl got out. The grass in front of the castle was grazed down like a lawn. She walked across to the massive front door and knocked loudly. Nothing happened. She stood back and considered, then walked round the down-hill side of the castle and disappeared through an archway in a high wall.

I waited for ages. The snow began to gather in a white line across the windscreen wipers. *Dear* Croydon, I thought.

But in a little while she came back.

"There's a fantastic old stableyard in there, in a courtyard behind the castle. And two really nice horses. And an old man who is going to go in the castle and open the front door for us. He said Mr. Robson is away tonight. He's gone to buy a stallion, coming back tomorrow. So we've got it all to ourselves, save for the housekeeper."

The housekeeper, Mrs. Melrose, was very old and stone-deaf. When the door opened she stood there to greet us, smiling. She looked like a black beetle in her dark clothes. She spoke with such a thick accent, neither of us could understand a word she said. But at least she smiled. The old man said he was the gardener. (What garden? I wondered.) He looked about a hundred, bent and gnarled, with only one tooth on the side at the front. His name was Willy, he said.

"I've worked here all me life. Born here I was. Long before this American chappie come. Worked for all the others. They come and go. No one stays here long."

"Why not?" asked Pearl.

Willy cackled with laughter.

"You'll see," he said. "Won't take long. The spirits don't rest easy here. No one's stayed save for a few years since the old family was all murdered by the reivers. That was a few hundred years ago, mind you, but the old place—it remembers."

"What's a reiver?" Pearl asked. She put her arm round my shoulders as she spoke, giving me a little squeeze. (In spite of all the moving, she's a good mother, I'll say that.)

"Border raiders, ma'am. It was all murder and mayhem in those days, stealing each other's cattle."

"Well, a few hundred years—that's a long time ago," Pearl said. "I don't think we need to worry about that today. All old houses—as old as this—have these stories to tell, don't they?"

She spoke briskly, in her usual no-nonsense, horsy way. It would take a pretty sharp ghost to frighten my mother. But no one with any sense, I thought, would stay here long, ghosts or no ghosts. Where was the nearest shop? School? Skateboard park? McDonald's?

We were led into a large stone-flagged hall with antlered deer heads staring down from the walls. It was freezing cold. A great stair-case rose up out of it to disappear into the dark above. But, thank goodness, we were ushered through a small dark door in a corner which led to the servants' quarters.

"There is where we live," said Willy.

An old-fashioned kitchen range glowed in a huge hearth, with pans bubbling interest-ingly on the hob. There was a big table with chairs round it and an enormous oak dresser.

No sign of shiny things like a washing machine or microwave or fridge. The floor was stone flags. There was a holey rug in front of the range on which lay a very old dog. It looked like a hound of some sort, but furry, with ragged ears and scars. It opened one eye, looked at us, sighed, and shut it again. The whole place was like something out of a Grimms' fairy tale.

But it was cozy and welcoming after the horrid outside. And Mrs. Melrose was already dishing up "soup." I thought she called it soup, but it was almost solid. In a large, black kettle she brewed tea and poured it into four mugs. Everything started to seem much more inviting. Of course I would have preferred fish fingers and chips, but I was so hungry, the soup seemed O.K.

In answer to Ma's questions, Willy gave us a rough idea of the setup. Mr. Robson had come to Scotland to research his ancestry. He boasted a Scottish forebear called Crackspear

Robson. Bloodybow had been Crackspear's home. He had bred horses—the "best in the land." The present Mr. Robson had found Bloodybow and bought it off the former owner. He was the first Robson to return to the family home since Crackspear died five hundred years ago.

"And very glad to be rid of it, the last man was," said Willy. "Thought he'd won the lottery! Fancy, this rich American appearing out of the blue and offering whatever he asked! He'd been trying to sell it all his life, ever since it was left to him in the will of his old auntie."

"And what does Mr. Robson intend to do here?" Pearl asked.

"He wants to breed horses, ma'am. He wants to breed the sort Crackspear bred—them old Galloways. 'E's got a bee in his bonnet, like."

"Galloways? Well, this is their home, the border country, where they used to breed them. Fast and strong, for raiding cattle! But they're extinct now—though there's still plenty of people breeding Fell ponies, which are the modern equivalent."

There's nothing my ma doesn't know about horses.

"Yeah, well, don't tell him that. He wants to improve the breed, 'e says. Like 'e's old Crackspear all over again. 'E's a bit of a romantic, like. Wants to play at being an old Border cattle raiser. 'E's read all the history."

"Well, it's a nice idea, improving a breed. It goes on all the time. If it keeps him happy, why not?"

"Old Crackspear—'e 'ad a stallion, a black stallion that was imported by King James from Hungary. He called it Flashing Steel. Don't ask me how 'e came by it, for no one knows. It was the most valuable horse in Britain, they said. Crackspear's neighbor, Walt o' Wideopen, stole the horse from him and spirited it away. Crackspear, 'e raided Wideopen and in his fury

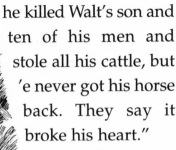

he killed Walt's son and ten of his men and stole all his cattle, but 'e never got his horse back. They say it broke his heart."

Cor! I thought.

"But this was a long time ago?" My mother tried to make it sound as if it didn't matter. Anything could have happened then.

"Five hundred years, thereabouts."

"It's all forgotten now, surely?"

Willy gave Ma a strange look, but did not answer. I thought that in a place like this, five hundred years was nothing. It was like five hundred years ago still. This kitchen could have been five hundred years ago.

So could my bedroom, when I was shown it.

It was in one of the towers and had round walls.
Dark crimson curtains
were closed across
the slitty windows,
and my fourposter
bed had matching

hangings. It was like being in a museum. But
rather magnificent. My bedroom! I had never
had anything like it in my life.

"My word!" Pearl was stroking the carving
on the oak pillars. "What have we come to? I
never expected anything like this!"

Her bedroom down the corridor was just
the same.

She kissed me good night and said, "I think this might be a lucky place, for a change! We'll see what it's like in the morning."

Chapter 2

I DIDN'T SLEEP very well, although I was so tired. Willy's story of the past history of Bloodybow went round and round in my head, helped—I swear—by the sound of hoofs galloping past outside. It was too cold to get out of bed and look. When my mother shook me awake at eight o'clock, I felt half-dead.

"I've been out and fed the mares. They're really nice. Great for you to ride. Mr. Robson is bringing the new stallion back today, from Glasgow, so we'll soon see if he knows anything about what to look for to breed good stock. With luck the man's got old Crackspear's genes."

Our boss sounded a nutter to me. Fancy giving up America for this creepy pile!

I shivered out of bed and put all my thickest clothes on—no one was going to see me out here!—and went down to the kitchen. Breakfast was porridge, as I might have guessed. But it was really nice, strangely, with creamy milk "straight from the coo," according to Willy. "We don't bother with any o' them newfangled laws up here," he said.

Afterwards I went out to the stableyard to see the ponies.

The yard was cobbled, the cobbles very worn. A lot of hoofs had passed this way. The stables were of thick stone, but had beautiful old mahogany linings and partitions, and the hay was still kept in the loft overhead, as it always had been.

The two mares were black Fell ponies without a speck of white on them. They had thick manes and tails and hairy legs, but their thick winter coats shone and they had the aura of quality that all good horses have. They were gentle and kind. Willy said their names were Black Rose and Lonely.

I was by myself in the stable, my mother having gone to see about feed. It was a long building, and I thought I heard the click of hoofs on the flagged floor at the far end. I walked curiously into what seemed the dim distance. To my surprise, right at the end was another pony. It was another mare, a Fell in type but snow-white. She was incredibly beautiful. She stood on a bed of straw, loose, without a bar to keep her in or a head collar to tie her up. She could have walked out if she liked.

The pony turned her lovely head and looked at me. It was very strange, but I some-how felt she wasn't real. So I went up to her and put my hand on her neck, and found she was warm and had the usual lovely horse smell I adored. I put my cheek against her white coat and she didn't turn away, but pushed her muzzle kindly at my hand.

"Oh, you are beautiful!"

A dream pony, I thought. Or perhaps—after all Willy's gruesome stories of the night before—a ghost pony.

I longed to try her out. But Willy had only mentioned two Fell mares. So who was this?

Willy was just coming in the door at the other end of the stables, carrying a bale of hay. I walked back and asked him. Willy dropped the bale and laughed.

"That's old Rowan."

"Old? How old?"

"She's been here ever since I can remember," Willy said. "And I can remember back to the day I was born."

"But you—you—"

He looked a hundred at least.

"Say seventy years," he said.

"No pony lives that long!"

"She's always been here. Since time was. I tell you,"—and he gave his crackling laugh—"there's things go on here you will never understand. And nor will the American gentleman. Not even me, save I got used to it all. I don't ask no questions, 'cause there aren't no answers."

What was I supposed to make of that?

I told my mother about Rowan, and she put her hand on my forehead and asked if I was feverish. She came and looked at the pony and was surprised to find one that no one had told her about, and said, "Of course she can't be that old."

She looked at the mare's teeth, to see how old she was.

"Well, old," she admitted. "But really—that Willy's a menace, making up these tales."

"Can I ride her? Try her out?"

"Why not? But remember," she laughed, "if she's seventy—go easy on her."

I RODE ROWAN that afternoon. She went like a dream. I had never ridden a pony like her before, and I have ridden plenty in my life. Her mouth was like silk, her stride so smooth and sweet that there was never a moment when you weren't at one with her, feeling part of her. She did what you asked before you asked, like she was reading your thoughts. She took me a way that I let her choose, because I knew it was safe. Don't ask me how I knew.

I knew she would bring me back before dark and take me the best path.

We went through the forest where the snow hadn't penetrated, noiseless along the soft, peaty paths. On Rowan I wasn't frightened, although without her I wouldn't have dreamed of going so deep away from home. And then, having ridden uphill for a long way, we came out on open, turfy ground and all the sea and the sky opened out before us, as if we were in a great theater with a back-cloth painted by God. Blue and sparkling, and the turf as if it had springs in it. Rowan cantered. I could hear the sea crashing on the rocks below the cliffs, and feel the cold, cold wind on my face, yet I was warm and my heart was singing as if I had never known what it was to ride a good pony.

I cannot explain it. Of course it was magic, literally.

It was like Willy said: there are things you will never understand.

But I stopped worrying then about McDonald's and things like that. Bloodybow was my place.

Chapter 3

*T*HAT AFTERNOON Mr. Robson arrived in a horsebox with his son Jed and the new stallion.

I felt very anxious, seeing the big, expensive horsebox lurching toward us.

"Crunch time," said my mother.

What would our new boss be like? And if Jed was a pain . . . !

The horsebox came to a halt, and Mr. Robson jumped down from the driver's seat. He came up to us with a smile and held out his hand.

"Mrs. Jenkins and Nicola? Pleased to meet you."

He was nice, you could see, not stuffy or arrogant. He introduced his son Jed, and I was relieved to see that he, too, looked O.K.— tousle-haired and a bit shy, about the same age as me. He said, "Hi."

"You'll have to put this lad to work, Mrs. Jenkins. He's not starting school until next September. There's not much in the way of entertainment up here, eh? Plenty to do though, getting it straight."

The stallion was kicking away now the box had stopped, so he went and let the ramp down.

My mother helped undo the partitions, and Mr. Robson led the horse out.

We had expected a Thoroughbred, but the horse was quite small, a very dark brown, very neat and proud and fiery and finely built.

"Well," said my mother, surprised. "What is he—an American breed?"

"That's right. He's a Morgan."

We had heard of Morgans, but not come

 across any in our travels. My mother was impressed.

"Very nice! He should make a good cross by the look of him."

"Yeah, that's what I thought. And they're hard as nails, Morgans. It's not putting softness in. He'll get tough stock, but with the quality."

Like the reivers had, I thought, for plundering and stealing and galloping away in the night. I shivered. I saw Jed look at me sideways.

While my ma and his father saw to installing the stallion, we trailed along behind.

"You like this place?" Jed asked.

I couldn't really answer. "It's strange. I don't know."

"Yeah, you can say that again. There's things happen in the night. Yeah, lights, screams sometimes. I tell my pa, and he says it's all in my imagination. These things happened once, not now. He says." Jed laughed. "And that weird pony at the end."

"Rowan?"

"Is that its name? Sometimes it disappears. Where to? My dad says it wasn't here when he bought the place. Then it turned up. And Willy said it belongs here. You can't make it out."

I said I'd ridden her. Jed was surprised.

"She was magic," I said.

"Oh, she's magic all right," said Jed.

I was really pleased that Jed agreed with me about the strangeness of Bloodybow—well, not exactly pleased, but glad that I was not alone in thinking there was something weird going on.

"We ought to ask that Willy what he knows," I suggested.

"I asked him," Jed said, "and he said it was because the Robsons have come back. That's us, you see. The feud was between the old

Robsons and the Armstrongs—it was an Armstrong called Walt of Wideopen that stole Crackspear's stallion, and Crackspear killed Walt's son to avenge it. The son was only young—ten, I think."

"Only ten! Willy didn't tell us that. How horrible!"

"But he was a wild boy—or so it said in the stuff my father read about it. He rode a stallion called Strongbow, which was the best in the Borders until Crackspear got his hands on Flashing Steel. That's the great one, the one all the fighting was about, the one they all wanted to possess. Fighting and killing—that's how it was in the Borders a long time ago. My dad's really keen on the history of it all. He's called our new stallion Crackspear's Stealaway and says he is going to breed the horses that Crackspear wanted to breed."

Jed paused and smiled. "He's a bit potty, my dad. Looking up this history—it's his great hobby."

Robson had made a fortune apparently, and had enough money to retire on. He wasn't going to go back to America.

"I wonder what those ghosts you've heard think of the new stallion," I said, half joking. "Do you think they want to steal it, like last time?"

Jed laughed then. "Don't be daft! How can they?"

But how could Rowan come and go? And be seventy years old? I was totally confused. But having Jed to share these thoughts with was a bonus.

"Does your father believe in these ghosts?" I asked.

"No. He said it's just in my mind. Too much imagination."

Like my ma.

IT WASN'T LONG before something very strange happened.

That evening we had a jolly supper round the table in the kitchen, Mr. Robson ("Call me

Rob, everybody does"), my mother, Jed, and me. There was a magnificent dining room in the cold part of the house, but Rob said, "That's not for us! In the summer perhaps, not now."

It was snowing again, rather more seriously this time, and the wind moaned in the forest. But inside by the glowing hearth it was cozy, with Willy bringing more logs and Mrs. Melrose finding wine in the cellar. Rob and my mother seemed to get on very well. The food was good—big homemade pies and roast potatoes— and Jed and I ate a lot. Bloodybow gave you an appetite.

Afterwards, Jed showed me his bedroom, which was just along from mine. He had a television and a computer and the Internet and heaven knows what else, but none of it worked very well, he said, because of the mountains and the forest all round. We managed to get the television showing a rather boring quiz program, then we went to bed.

My head was going round. There was a lot to think about, and my mother had let me have a glass of wine, too. But I slept eventually. All was silent.

I don't know what time I woke. It was still dark. And quiet. What had woken me?

Then I heard it—a horse whinnying from the stableyard.

I jumped out of bed. Horses don't whinny in the night for nothing, even if they are in a new place. I ran to the window and looked down into the yard.

The whinny came again. I was sure this time it was Stealaway. There was a light bobbing below by the archway, nothing else. But whose light?

While I was standing there, heart thumping, my door opened with a creak.

I squeaked.

But—"It's only me," said Jed.

He came across to the window. "Did you hear Stealaway?"

"Yes. What's frightening him?"

We stood together, looking down. It was snowing quite hard, and the snow had drifted into the stableyard so that it was quite deep against the floor of the stable block. The light now moved through the archway and into the yard, and was joined by another, and then another. Yet they shone only on pristine snow. They seemed to have no person holding them, no footsteps following them. I think Jed was as scared as I was.

The stallion's voice rang out again—a frightened horse.

As we watched, there was a sudden movement, and Rowan appeared in the stable doorway. She stood foursquare, gleaming in the snow, silver against white. She seemed suddenly much bigger, very strong.

The three lights stopped. They circled the doorway.

Yet there was nobody there!

Rowan struck out with a foreleg, and we saw the snow fly up. She reared and dropped down again, striking at one of the lights. The light whirled and fell back. She reared up again, striking out, and again and again, launching her flashing hoofs at the lights. The lights shook and grew pale. They fell back, fading perceptibly, blinking and then disappearing altogether. The yard was still and silent.

And Rowan had disappeared.

Stealaway was quiet. All was peaceful. The snow lay smooth and unblemished.

We knew, somehow, that all was well. We felt calm, the shivers finished.

"Whatever it was, she protected him," Jed whispered.

"Whatever it was—but what was it?"

But even Willy had said there were no answers.

"Does it happen every night?" I asked. "We could lie out there one night and keep watch. Stealaway saw something."

But we made no plans, not much liking the idea.

We went back to bed. But I did not sleep again. The snow had stopped and a bright moon shone, and when I looked out it was very peaceful. A large hare lolloped across the drive.

In the morning when we went out, the sun was shining. Stealaway was calmly eating the remains of his hay.

There was no sign of Rowan. The snow lay thick in the yard, yet there were no hoof-prints.

"Where did she go?" Jed whispered.

"Maybe the spirits took her!"

We asked Willy. But all he would say was, "You can rest easy if Rowan's not here. She'll be back if trouble's brewing."

I wanted her back so badly! But I didn't want trouble.

Chapter 4

THE NEXT FEW weeks passed uneventfully. After the initial frights and with Rowan gone, Jed and I wondered if we had been dreaming about what we had seen and heard in the night. But nobody dreams the same dream as someone else, surely?

My mother didn't expect me to go to school right away. She said wait till September, when Jed would go. I knew it was miles even to the school bus stop and she hated ferrying, so that was great by me. And Jed and I got on well. We rode out in the mornings on the two mares, Black Rose and Lonely, and my mother came on Stealaway, and afterwards we messed about, building a tree house or damming the stream, and things like that. If it was wet, we messed about in Jed's room. We were supposed to educate ourselves on the Internet, but of course we only played games or looked for things we weren't supposed to. We didn't get bored.

Stealaway got the two mares in foal, but of course we would have to wait nearly a year for the foals to be born. In the meantime we could have great fun riding. We put up jumps in the grazing field and made a cross-country course through the woods using fallen trees and old hurdles and things. Rob and my ma liked us using the mares, keeping them fit, and my mother doted on Stealaway. In his summer coat, with my mother's grooming and care, he looked a real winner. His coat was very dark with faint golden mottles, and he had a beautiful head with bold, intelligent eyes. His action was smooth and straight. I rode him sometimes and loved it. But neither he nor my mare, Black Rose—Rosie—nor Jed's mare, Lonely, were a patch on Rowan. I longed to see her again.

Rob was away quite a bit, "winding up things" in the States, but when he was home, he wandered around a lot researching the Robsons

and the border feuds. One day he rode out on Stealaway with Jed and me and said he had something to show us. We usually rode through the woods and out onto the cliffs because it was so lovely, but this time we rode in the other direction, down the valley, the way we had driven up. We took the turning marked Hanging Law, and the ride took us into a narrow valley with crags and forest on either side. After a while the valley opened out into a wide bowl of wind-seared grass. It was as bleak and horrid a spot as you could possibly find. In the middle was a broken stone tower, a sort of castle with only slits for windows high up, and one door below.

"This is Wideopen," Rob said. "Walt's home."

We pulled up and sat looking. It was a gray day, and even now in summer a bitter wind blew down on us from the hillside ahead. Nobody, I thought, could be happy in a place like this, even if the sun was shining.

Rob got off Stealaway and led us to a patch of sheep-grazed grass near the castle door. A big flagstone showed in the grass, much worn. It had something chiseled on it, old letters but quite indecipherable. The only recognizable thing was a cross at the top.

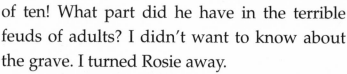

"Somebody told me that this is the child's grave—Walt's son, that Crackspear killed," Rob said.

I hated this story. A child of ten! What part did he have in the terrible feuds of adults? I didn't want to know about the grave. I turned Rosie away.

"It's horrible!"

I nearly said I was glad I wasn't a Robson. Poor child, lying in this terrible place! Rosie broke into a trot as if she, too, wanted to be away from this beastly castle.

Rob mounted, and we rode away gratefully.

He said, "There was never peace in those days, once a feud started between families. All that killing over a horse! And it seems the horse, Flashing Steel, never became Walt's anyway, because it disappeared after he stole it. There is a legend that he could be seen running wild over the hills, with a little white mare at his side. But no one could ever catch them."

I didn't dare look at Jed, my heart jolted so hard. A little white mare!

Rowan! Rowan, the protector, Rowan, my darling, magic mare!

Rob obviously didn't make the connection. To him Rowan was just a pensioned-off pet of Willy's who went missing on the moor most of the time. But he hadn't ridden her. He didn't know she was magic.

Rob went on talking to Jed about something else historical—he could be quite boring sometimes—and I rode behind on my own, feeling the cold wind blowing down from

Wideopen like a steely breath on my back, bidding me depart. There was no welcome at Wideopen, nor had there ever been.

But Rowan had known Flashing Steel.

WHEN WE GOT back to the stable, we took the horses inside to unsaddle them before we turned them out in the field.

And Rowan stood in her place at the far end, eating out of the manger.

It surely was no coincidence, after our visit to Wideopen. Why on earth did Rob want to uncover these ghosts that lay so uneasily in their graves? And what had Willy said?

"You can rest easy if Rowan's not here. She'll be back if trouble's brewing."

I saw Jed was thinking the same as me, his eyes out on stalks at the sight of her. Yes, there were things at Bloodybow that could not be explained, in spite of Rob thinking he had all the answers. These ghosts needed laying to rest, or none of us would remain safe. But how to fight ghosts? I had no idea.

Chapter 5

BUT NOTHING HAPPENED.
    I rode Rowan again, and she gave me the same fantastic feel. But when Jed tried to ride her, she would not move. When he tried to make her, she bucked him off, in spite of his being such a good rider. I asked Willy why she had come back, although I knew the answer.

"Oh, that's the way of her," he said. "When she feels the spirits rising, she comes back to Bloodybow."

"Where is she when she isn't at Bloody-bow?"

"I reckon she's with them old ones, Crack-spear's Flashing Steel."

Of course, Willy was completely potty. But after what Rob had told us, it fitted—if one believed in ghosts. Which at that time I still thought I didn't. Was it possible that the two horses were still to be seen together, galloping side by side over the dark hills?

I couldn't make head or tail of it. Nor could Jed.

"The man's completely cracked. I reckon your mother's right, that he takes Rowan away somewhere himself. None of it makes sense."

No. We had been lulled by the summer and our pleasant life, riding and messing about and not having to go to school. But why was Rowan back? Because the spirits were rising . . . But with the long, light nights and the soft blue skies, the whirring of midges and the song of the thrush in the pines, our memory of the lanterns in the snowy yard had faded.

We made camp in the horses' field. Now summer had come, the horses were out in the field all night and in the cool of the stable out of the midges in the daytime. Jed had a super-duper state-of-the-art tent that blew up with a pump, and I had a terrible old one-man thing my mother had had in her Girl Guide days. We set them up side by side and made a fire and cooked sausages. I had a mothy old sleep-

ing bag, and Jed had one that had cost two hundred pounds. It was too hot, of course, and he slept on top and got bitten by midges. Luckily, none of the horses were bothered with us and they were too sensible to get caught up in the guy lines. They grazed in a

group, the two black mares, beautiful Steal-away and, slightly apart, Rowan like a silver ghost. (Or was she a silver ghost?)

The field had been cleared from the forest and lay below the castle, fenced, with forest below it. The gate was opposite the stableyard.

Willy said, "You be careful now."

"What of?" I said.

But he only said, "Rowan will guard you."

"He really is cracked," Jed said.

One night it was rather windy, and Rob said, "Maybe you should sleep indoors tonight. Your tent might blow away."

Jed groaned.

"Nicky's tent more likely," my mother said. "But I suppose a tree might fall on them."

"We're well out of the trees!"

They didn't argue. We thought it was fun. The tents were certainly rather lively, but after all, if they did blow away, we only had to run for the stout embrace of Bloodybow. No storm would ever threaten those walls.

I turned in and lay listening to the wind in the trees. Rowan, unusually, had left the others and was grazing quite nearby. I could see her shadow, long in the evening sun. (At least she had a shadow. Did ghosts have shadows?) The light was strange, both gold and yet dusk, and already, far over the black pines in the crags above, a half-moon was shining. It came and went, the clouds flying. I lay thinking how lucky we had landed up, my mother and I. She got on with Rob and found him an easy boss, and Jed was great. He was quite grown-up in his ways, didn't say much, but was very good-natured. He was a great rider, too. He had ridden ever since he could remember. Like me. At least we had one good skill each, even if we were getting a bit behind with our maths and modern languages.

So I lay thinking nice thoughts, and then I realized the wind was rising with a vengeance. The trees were bending and cracking and making a howling noise all round us, and my tent was bucking like a horse. The light was very strange, the moon still shining through a gauze of flying thundercloud, coming and going.

I looked out. The horses were standing with their ears pricked up, very nervous. Horses don't usually bother much with weather, even thunder and lightning. I couldn't see Rowan. I looked across at Jed's tent, and of course, unlike mine, it was as steady as a rock, the best the United States could produce. He was probably sound asleep.

I put my head down, trying not to imagine things. My pillow was a skinny thing with only a few feathers between me and the ground, and when I lay flat with my ear to the ground, I could feel a sort of trembling beneath me. It was very weird. The ground was solid rock a few inches down. How could it tremble? But there was a rhythm to it that I recognized— galloping hoofs.

This had happened to me once before when camping, when some cows had got into the field, and I remembered hearing the thud of their hoofs when my ear was to the ground. But cows are one thing . . . galloping horses . . . ? I moved my pillow and put my ear flat to the turf. This time there was no doubt. The sound was much nearer, and coming fast. I tried to pretend it was the wind, the rolling of thunder, but I could not stop a great sweat of fear suddenly burning over me. This was what happened at Bloodybow—killing and mayhem! We had more than enough proof.

I put my head out and screamed, "Jed!"

He peered out. "What's up? Is your tent O.K.?"

I tried to keep the panic out of my voice.

"Yes. But put your ear to the ground and listen!"

He had been reading by torchlight, but now he did what I told him. The next minute he stuck his head out.

"Hey—wow! Let's get out of here!"

As he spoke, Rowan came cantering up the field toward us. She looked like a white flame running over the grass. She swept up to our tents and stood in front of us, head up, nostrils dilated. She looked mighty—not in size, but in presence. I cannot explain how exactly. She

seemed to shine with an unearthly light, and her eyes directed us distinctly. "Get on," they said. No messing.

We needed no further bidding. The sound of approaching hoofs were all mixed now with rolls of thunder, and the tents were about to take off in the blasts of wind. Rowan stood like a rock. Jed gave me a leg-up and vaulted up behind me and Rowan leapt straight into a gallop and sped away down the field toward the far fence.

Stealaway stood there with his mares, all eyes and twitching ears. The trees behind him tossed and groaned in the wind. We slid off Rowan—tumbled, more like—and rolled under the fence like startled rabbits.

I was terrified. For the hoofs were there now, bearing down on Bloodybow. The whole ground shook. Our tents seemed to fly up in the air, plucked by an invisible hand. Shapes spinning, the sound of steel clashing, and terrible groans . . . and then one figure detached itself from the whirling shadows and came toward us.

I cannot describe it. It was neither real nor unreal: a shape only, transparent and unearthly. Yet there was nothing unreal about the presence, the stench of death. There was blood on the figure, small and lithe, blood on the horse, and terrible eyes, dying. The horse was a chestnut, very dark, with a thick knotted mane, only small but built like a tank. Its eyes were fireballs, sparks flew from its heels. It reared up, making for Stealaway, but Rowan swung round and stood in its path.

I have never seen a braver horse than Rowan. She was all teeth and laid-back ears, laying into the chestnut horse. She turned and battered him with her heels, swirled back with gnashing teeth, reared up and slashed out with her forelegs. You could hear the terrible thud of her hoofs on hard flesh, the rip of muscle, tearing breath.

Yet the chestnut horse did not turn and flee.

It stood its ground. It was a little war-horse, muddy and sweaty, with a mane tangled with filth that hung to its shoulder. I could see its eyes burning, and the stubbornness and the courage. Its head was up, ears pricked. And I thought Rowan, the mare, did not have the same strength. It was like attacking a tree trunk. But how she attacked!

The chestnut horse, set fast, did not turn, but faded. One moment I could see clearly enough to make out the sweat and blood pouring down the shoulder, the wet curls of the thick, exhausted coat. I could see the child rider with the sword through his chest and the dead eyes. And the next minute they had vanished.

THE FIGHT WAS over. I stared and stared, hypnotized by the sight of the dead rider, but there was no sign of anything there. Had there ever been?

I put my head down in the grass. I was

shaking uncontrollably, as if I was Rowan herself. I know I was crying. The vision was so sharp and so terrible, yet—when I opened my eyes and looked up—it was only the familiar field, the wind now softly soughing in the pines. All the fury had gone.

And the horses . . . the horses were grazing, Rowan close by Stealaway. But her coat was all sweaty and her flanks heaved.

I put my head in my arms. It was unbearable, what I had seen. Under my head the echo of the hoofs in the peaty earth shuddered, receding. They were going back down the valley toward Wideopen, fainter and fainter. Was

that little horse with them, carrying his terrible burden? I was crying, shaking. I knew what I had seen—or felt—yet these things didn't happen. But it wasn't a dream. I hadn't even been asleep.

"Jed?" I croaked.

"Holy cow!" he whispered. He put his arm across my shoulders and gave me a little shake. "You saw all that?"

"Yes!"

"It wasn't just—it was for real?"

"Yes. To me it was."

"And me."

We slowly got ourselves together, stood up. My knees were shaking. I went over to Rowan and put my arms around her, laid my cheek against her sweat-soaked neck.

"You saved our lives, Rowan."

But now she was just an ordinary pony, exhausted, it seemed, for no apparent reason, just grazing in a twilit field. Stealaway kept close to her. The field was now serene, the wind dropped and the trees still. The sky was full of stars. We left the horses and walked slowly back to the mess where our tents had been. They were in a tangled heap. Jed pulled his ruined American beauty into shape on the grass. It was badly torn. He picked up his sleeping bag and a cloud of feathers (it was pure goose down, of course) flew up in the air. It had one tear in it, right across the middle,  so that it was almost in two halves.

"A sword did that," Jed said. His voice shook. He would have been in two halves too, had he not run for it.

We contemplated the mess, speechless.

"I think we'd better go back in the castle," he said shakily.

We were too done in to try and make up explanations. No one would believe our story, so we crept up to bed to sleep it off.

Chapter 6

I THOUGHT ROWAN would disappear, the spirits having departed, but she didn't. She was there the next morning, grazing quietly by Stealaway's side.

My mother thought she looked peaky.

"Her age is catching up with her," she said.

Yes, I thought, five hundred is pretty old. Dear Rowan, who had saved our lives!

In the morning by light of day and after a sleep of deep, stunned exhaustion, it was amazing how the events of the night before no longer seemed so shocking. Like a dream, the image had receded. Of course there was a logical explanation . . . we would work it out eventually.

Jed and I convinced ourselves that one could not be killed by the slash of a ghost's sword. We laughed. Rob and my mother laughed at the mess of our tents, and we said the sleeping bags had blown into the thorn-bushes and got torn. They didn't bother to look very hard. They thought it was all quite funny and obviously hadn't heard a thing. Rob said he was going to Edinburgh to meet a historian who knew more about Walt of Wideopen and the son killed by Crackspear.

Jed said, edgily, "Why don't you give it a rest, Dad?"

Rob looked surprised, slightly hurt.

"Why, what harm does it do?"

We couldn't tell him, of course. They would

never believe us! We scarcely believed it ourselves.

When they had gone we discussed it.

"The little chestnut that Rowan attacked—that was Strongbow and his rider was Walt's son."

"Yes. They are jealous—that we have a lovely stallion again and are breeding horses like old Crackspear did. How can we get rid of them?"

"We beat them. Beat them enough times and they'll give up," said Jed.

"But how many times?"

I didn't fancy the prospect at all.

"We'll know we've won when Rowan goes."

"I can't bear for Rowan to go!" I said.

"When she goes for good, we'll be safe."

"Poor Rowan, protecting us! She's old and tired!" Funny how you could say these things, as if it was all real. Yet Jed knew, too. It wasn't just me.

"They came for Stealaway," Jed said. "But they were seen off. They will try again, I'm sure. We'll have to keep a good watch on him."

Rob said, when he came back from Edinburgh, "The blood feuds were so vicious, they haunt the place still. You only have to stand here alone, on a dark night, and I swear you can hear the riders coming and hear the screams."

Jed and I looked at each other.

"Yes," we said.

"Now what?" I said to Jed afterwards.

"We wait and see what happens next. Stealaway will be taken and my father will go nuts."

"How will they take him?"

"If it's jealousy, they will kill him. They don't want him, after all—only for us not to have him."

"But how?"

"That remains to be seen."

But not for long.

When you least expect it, I remember thinking. How right I was!

Chapter 7

IT WAS A very hot day in August. All had been quiet—idyllic. Jed and I knew that school was looming. I suppose, in a way, we were both quite looking forward to it—something new, new friends and all that—but it meant we were savoring our freedom now.

Rob and Ma had gone to get building stuff for the castle—Rob worked on it more or less full-time—and Jed and I were alone. We thought we would go for a lazy ride through the woods and up on to the cliffs where the sea breeze would cool us. Rowan was still with us, and I rode her all the time now. No other horse in the world could touch her for the pure pleasure she gave—to me, at least—and somehow I knew I wouldn't have her forever. The fact that she hadn't gone away was in one way a nightmare. Jed and I were on eternal lookout for the evils from Wideopen, but as the days passed we began to relax. I treasured riding Rowan while I could. I did not want it spoiled.

"Ma said put the horses in till evening when it cools down," I said.

So Stealaway and Black Rose were shut in their boxes in the cool of the stable and Jed and I rode off on Rowan and Lonely.

Rowan was very nervous. I could feel tremors running through her, and she was hating the dark woods, shying occasionally at shadows. Her nervousness transferred to me.

"Something's wrong," I said. "I can feel it in Rowan."

But Jed said, "Oh, come on, it's the heat. She'll settle out on the cliffs. We'll be able to breathe up there."

Strange how cloying the heat was in this
northern place, thick in the woods, loud with
the humming of insects. I trotted on and the
ground started rising, the trees thinning. The
sky was a great coppery bowl ahead, the whole
canopy of it which we so rarely saw down in
the Bloodybow valley. Rowan broke into a can-
ter and we pounded up the springy turf
toward the edge of the cliffs. Jed came more
steadily, Lonely being in foal.

I knew something was wrong. There was a
strange smell in the air—not the clear scent of

the sea, but something thick that caught in the throat. I pulled up at the top of the ride, and Rowan suddenly swung round, facing back the way we had come, and whinnied.

Far away, where Bloodybow was, a column of smoke was rising out of the trees. It wasn't a lazy column like a woodman's fire, but a wild, vicious twirling of spitting fire. I almost thought I could hear the crack of it. It plumed triumphantly above the forest, twisting as it went like an angry serpent, spreading its foul smell across the sky.

And Stealaway and Black Rose were shut in the stable!

Willy and Mrs. Melrose had gone to town. Ma and Rob were away. And we—we were seven or eight miles away. Impossible to get back . . .

"Rowan!" I whispered. "Please . . ."

I don't know what I expected, only that she wouldn't let me down. She took off like a scalded cat and her power flowed into my own body so that there was no way I was ever going to fall off, in spite of her speed. Did she fly, did she spirit the trees away? I had no idea, only that the thick forest seemed to fall apart before us; the trees bowed down, the glades opened up and we went through them like a tearing wind. I lay crouched on her neck, my hands knotted in her flying mane. I was part of her, my heart and her heart were one—we were one animal.

The awful stink of burning and evil enfolded us as Bloodybow's walls reared up ahead. The stables were on fire. I had known it all along. As we came through the archway I saw the flames pouring out of the door and the

windows. No horse could come out of that alive! I am not brave. I tried. I leapt off and ran to the door, but the heat made it impossible. It threw me back like a punch, and with it I felt the malevolence— no ordinary fire this, but an eruption of hate— shouting in my face. Laughing, winning, beating us. I put my hand out to reach the door latch, but it was impossible. I turned back.

"Stealaway!" I screamed. "Rowan, save him! Save him! And Black Rose is in there, too!"

But Rowan was no longer alone. Another horse stood there.

In all the smoke and confusion—and my eyes were streaming tears so I could hardly

see—there was a beautiful young mare, silver gray, and a black stallion. Oh, what a stallion! Framed by fire, his coat was burnished with gold, his eyes burnt flame, his wild black tail swirled amongst the flying sparks. Contained energy sprung from his presence—a power that dazzled. Nothing could touch him, no ghost from Wideopen, no vengeful sword! And in his presence Rowan had returned to her youth, all her years shed, a pony of exquisite beauty, a perfect match for the magnificent horse she served.

Rowan had summoned Flashing Steel to save us!

All my fear dissolved. I went to the door again and this time the bolts were cool to my hand. I opened the door and went in. An archway of cool air met me and led me to the inside box where Stealaway lived. He stood there on the burning straw, yet was untouched, head up, trembling. I opened the door and reached for his head collar. He did not panic, but came with me, then stood whilst I released Black Rose. I led them back to the door, and they came like angels—no panic, no fear. I let them out into the yard.

As I did so, the stables erupted in fire behind me with a roar. A wave of flame reached out for me like hellfire, and I ran blindly. I heard the clatter of hoofs on the cobbles all around me, but couldn't see for smoke. My eyes were streaming. The heat was intense.

Oh, how those stables burned! They burned with the fury of thwarted rage, devouring the empty boxes. The flames writhed into the sky, the hay in the roof dissolved in a black fallout like the devil's own funeral ashes, and the smoke made a cloud so big that it completely blotted out the sun. The stone walls blackened but stood. The rest dissolved. Consumed. Every vestige of the old—the beautiful mahogany, the cracked mangers, the silky-smooth partitions polished by centuries of horses' soft coats—all that history, that dreadful history, eaten up in flame. The roof crashed in with a roar and fountains of flying sparks exploded into the sky.

With the horses saved I felt exultant. Burn, burn, burn! The fire would cleanse that terrible history, cauterize the pain, banish the ghosts. I watched it, gloating, loving the heat that even as I watched forced me to retreat. I knew the castle walls were inviolate. But the stable-yard—let it go. I went out through the archway onto the grass, to find relief for my aching body.

And on the forecourt of the ancient castle the old stallion and the new for a moment were touching noses, at peace. I was struck by

their similarity. Dear Stealaway was a miniature of the great Flashing Steel, the same dark coat burnished with golden mottles, the proud eye and presence, the same great heart. And as I watched—maybe because I watched— Flashing Steel suddenly reared, flung round, and galloped away down the road, Rowan at his side.

I knew I was never going to see them again. Rowan was surely going home now to where she belonged, to where she should have rested hundreds of years before. I was desperate not to lose her, not to let her dissolve as Strongbow had dissolved. I wanted to see more of Flashing Steel, who would never come again. And in my desperation I turned to Stealaway, standing by the gate.

He seemed to know what I wanted, for he stood like a rock while I jumped onto the gate and slid my leg over his back. Then, without a sign from me, he was away down the road in pursuit. I had no saddle and he wore only a

 head collar, but he needed no aids from me to tell him what to do. He knew. And I knew now that Stealaway was a worthy successor to Flashing Steel, his action so free and light, with speed to match. Maybe the Armstrong ghosts had only been aroused to such evil because they recognized his worth and his similarity. Our American Mr. Robson had unknowingly followed Crackspear's path in arousing the mad Armstrong jealousy.

Stealaway swung up the side road marked to Hanging Law. I was ready for him, holding tight with my knees, and swung with him. What a wonderful stride he had! Lengthening as he met the hill, he covered the ground like a racehorse. I knew I would never ride Rowan again, but at this moment I swore I would change my allegiance to Stealaway and be as happy. He gave me the same feel, the feel that only special horses give of wanting to be at one with the rider—giving, pleasing.

We came back to the bleak, bare bowl of Wideopen and saw the old bones of the castle standing against the summer sky. We slowed, but did not stop, cantering easily past and up the far slope. The turf was sheep-grazed close, and seemed to spring under the silent hoofs. I had never come up here before.

The hill steepened, and Stealaway snorted. He ducked his head and sprang up the last crest, and I held a handful of mane to stop from sliding back.

At the top, bare blue hills and moorland spread for miles to a far, far distant horizon, hazed by the heat of summer and the smoke from Bloodybow. The ground was all heather and turf—great raiding ground, fast and sure underfoot. Wideopen was well placed, broaching this fine, wild landscape.

This was Flashing Steel's pasture, where it was said he had been seen galloping with the little silver mare at his side. And this was what I saw now, granting my fervent wish. Away in the blue distance they were still going, tireless, timeless, tails streaming. To me at that moment they were real—as real as my own horse under me who could see them too. For he put up his head and whinnied. And, almost out of sight, the little mare stopped in her stride and turned back to look, and perhaps—*perhaps*—I heard

the echo of a farewell call. How could I ever be sure? And then, side by side, they disappeared, faded, into the heat haze.

And I knew I would never see either of them again.

Chapter 8

WELL, HOW TO explain all that?

I told Jed, of course, and we made up a story for Ma and Mr. Robson. Not lies, just leaving a lot of things out. Of course, they were so grateful the horses were safe, they didn't bother about too many details. I told them we got back in time to get the horses out, before the flames really took hold. Very hard to say why we hadn't rung the fire brigade, but as the telephone often didn't work, the line coming up so far amongst the pine trees, they didn't press us on this point.

In fact, Mr. Robson, surveying the damage,

said, "Perhaps it did us a good turn, after all. It will be great to build new stables, all the mod cons. We're a new enterprise, starting a new line. We don't want to feel bound to the past."

"You are a fine one to talk, Dad," Jed scoffed.

"Yes, well, I had a bit of a bee in my bonnet about all that old history, but I've found out all I need to know. I'm going to give it a rest now, look to the future. What a lot of work ahead of us—but what fun, planning it all!"

"Well, I must say, I didn't care for those old buildings," my mother said. "Bad ventilation, dark and stuffy. If we could build new we could—"

And they were away, the two of them, making plans, arguing, laughing.

Jed and I looked at each other.

"Good-bye, history," said Jed. "Thank heaven for that!"

Good-bye, Rowan, I thought. Good-bye, ghosts!

But, like my mother, I felt excitement for the future blotting out my regrets. Jed, Stealaway, even school . . . the best things were all ahead of us, and Bloodybow could have a future, too, not just a past.